BRONSON BEAVER
BUILDS A ROBOT

Written by
TEKO BERNARD

Illustrated by Howard Russell

PUBLISHING

ISBN COMPLETE: 978-0-9860593-6-0
ISBN/SKU: 9780986059360

All rights reserved. Published by Tabron Publishing.

Printed in the United States of America.

Written by Teko Bernard
Illustrated by Howard Russell
Designed by Teko Bernard

Contents

For the brave
and imaginative
dream-builders
everywhere.

—CHAPTER 1—
BEAVER VALLEY LODGE

Hidden somewhere deep within the Great Forest lived Bronson Beaver, a small and industrious thirteen-year-old aspiring inventor, with messy brown fur, an imagination as big as the baggy red hoodie he wore, and the determination of, well...a beaver. Bronson loved to do two things: build cool stuff and hang out with his best friends, Franny Fox and Myron Mink.

Bronson lived with his parents in a massive twelve-room, two-story log cabin called the Beaver Valley Lodge. Surrounded by a web of gurgling streams, snow-capped mountains, towering pine trees, and lush green meadows, the Beaver Valley Lodge was not only Bronson's home, but also the central hub of the most popular wilderness resort in the world. It was visited each year by a parade of wild and eccentric adventurers seeking its fresh air, dream-like vistas, never-ending hiking trails, and sparkling salmon-filled waters.

Owned and operated by Bronson's family for over 150 years, the Beaver Valley Lodge was originally designed and built by Bronson's pioneering ancestor, Barrett van Beaver, who wanted to help protect his furry brethren in the forest by providing them a safe refuge from the harsh winters. The lodge itself and the surrounding wooded acres of Beaver Valley soon became a family heirloom to be passed down through the generations. Bronson's parents, who were now in charge of managing the lodge and maintaining the land, would one day pass it down to Bronson and his future family.

But until that day, Bronson was responsible for helping with any odd jobs around the lodge and providing maintenance for the lodge's complex network of century-old dams.

But Bronson didn't want to be stuck in the same neck of the woods his whole life, following in his elders' webbed footsteps of managing an old lodge. No, instead Bronson dreamed wildly about becoming a great inventor and getting out of the woods of Beaver Valley to explore the world, which wasn't really all that wild of a dream because Bronson indeed was a remarkable inventor and master builder with a gift for creating just about anything he could imagine.

However, with his ever-increasing number of new responsibilities around the lodge, Bronson felt like he never had any free time to hang out with his friends anymore. But that was about to change because Bronson was about to make his most brilliant invention ever, which was sure to change his life and allow him to have more fun with his friends and do less tedious work around the lodge.

– CHAPTER 2 –
WHAT'S THE BIG IDEA?

It all started one warm spring evening. After finishing dinner and his final chores of the day, Bronson raced to his bedroom, closed the door, launched his favorite video chat app on his desktop, and called up his two best friends. Franny and Myron quickly answered and popped up on his computer screen in separate windows, eagerly waiting to play their favorite video game, Zombie Fight.

Bronson's gamer buddies were also tech-savvy, aspiring inventors like him. Franny Fox was a soft-spoken coder with a big bright smile, bushy orange tail, and a love for writing apps and wearing flannel shirts and knit beanies.

Myron Mink was a loud and hyperactive mechanical-gadget-building expert with stark white fur and a long skinny neck, who wore an old grease-stained trucker hat and mechanic shirt like a badge of honor. And whenever all three of them worked together, they were an unstoppable creative force from nature.

"You ready to play, bro?" asked Myron.

"Yeah! Are you all done with your chores?" asked Franny.

"Yes, FINALLY!" Bronson replied.

"Sweet, let's do this!" screamed Myron.

"Let's do this!" Bronson yelled back while untangling his headset cord.

Zombie Fight was hosting a big weekend tournament to kick off the latest version of the game, and Bronson and his pals were one of fifty teams invited to play. They hoped to win the cash prize to help them finally build their dream workshop where they could have a place to hang out together and develop their inventions.

But just before Bronson could plug in his headset, his father, Barry, knocked on the door before shuffling into Bronson's room. Barry was mild-mannered and as conservative as the khaki pants and cardigan sweaters he liked to wear. He was slightly taller and rounder than Bronson, with lighter brown carefully-groomed fur, small round glasses, and the assuredness of, well…a beaver.

"Bronson, make sure you get to bed early tonight. We have a lot of work to do tomorrow."

"But tomorrow is Saturday. It's my only day to hang out and play video games with my friends," Bronson replied.

"Yes, but we have to get ready for the Pancake Festival on Sunday."

"Oh, no! Is that this weekend?"

With so much hype about the video game tournament, Bronson had forgotten about the lodge's annual Pancake Festival, a grand event hosted at the lodge each spring. It was the oldest and largest pancake festival in the world, and everyone living in and around Beaver Valley showed up to the lodge's restaurant, The Bear Claw, for their award-winning pancake breakfast, and Bronson was partly responsible.

It was his invention, the Pancake Maker Pro, that helped them set a world record for making seventy-six thousand pancakes in eight hours and serving seventeen thousand customers.

"Yes, this Sunday, Bronson," Barry said, "and this year we're being judged by world-renowned food critic, Bardo J. Bear from the *Good Grub Gazette,* so we need to be sure everything is perfect! Here is the list of projects you need to complete by tomorrow. So don't stay up too late playing video games."

BRONSON'S CHORES

1. Chop the firewood
2. Sweep the porch
3. Clean the gutters
4. Paint the welcome sign
5. Cut the grass
6. Clean and organize the toolshed
7. Patch and inflate the raft
8. Fix the hot tub
9. Clean the BBQ pit
10. Mend the fence

Barry handed him a sheet of paper with a very long list and hurried back out of his room, closing the door behind him.

"Seriously!" Bronson grimaced and turned the list around for his friends to see. "Look at this list!"

"BRO! There is no way you'll get all of that done before the tournament starts tomorrow morning," said Myron.

"Myron is right, Bronson. We need you if we're going to have a chance to win," said Franny.

"Bro, if we can't depend on you to play, we will need to find another person to replace you," Myron said.

"No way!" Bronson protested.

Bronson didn't want to let his friends down or get replaced with a new teammate. And to top it off, he badly wanted to win the money so they could afford to build the bigger workshop they so desperately needed. But his friends were right. It would be impossible for him to finish all his work before the tournament started. But what could he do? It wasn't fair. He would have to be a machine to complete all those projects.

"Wait, that's it!" Bronson said.

"What's it?" Franny asked.

"I have an idea!" Bronson exclaimed.

"Well, let's hear it," Myron said.

"I may not be a machine, but what if I build a machine to help me?"

"You mean like a robot?" Franny asked.

"Exactly!" Bronson said with a giant smile. "I'm going to build a robot and program it to go out and do all of my chores tomorrow so I can stay inside and play Zombie Fight!"

"Are you kidding me?" Myron said. "That's brilliant!"

"Just give me one night to build it, and I'll be ready to play tomorrow." And with that, Bronson grabbed his laptop and ran out of his bedroom with excitement.

"Good, because we can't win the game without you!" Franny shouted.

"I know—I won't let you down!" Bronson shouted back.

— CHAPTER 3 —
THE ROBOT

B ronson quietly moseyed past his parents, who were busy downstairs discussing the Pancake Festival, and hustled outside to the old toolshed behind the lodge. The toolshed was a dark, cramped, and dusty space packed tightly with a massive pile of old junk on one side and a stockpile of freshly chopped wood on the other. The toolshed was where Bronson and his friends tried to work on their inventions. But it was proving to be too small and crowded now, which was a big reason why they wanted to build a totally new space.

The woodpile in the workshop included a variety of maple, aspen, and willow wood, which had all been cut down, debarked, and gathered by Bronson himself. Most of the wood was used for repairing the lodge and nearby dams, but Bronson and his friends also used it—along with the junk parts—to make their inventions.

Myron was responsible for discovering most of the random items in the junk pile. Since he lived down in the valley close by the Town Market, and was the only one from the trio with a vehicle or license to drive, he would frequently patrol the alleys and back streets of all the merchants' shops and residents' dwellings in the village, hunting for any discarded materials that his wild imagination fancied, which was just about *everything*.

Bronson didn't have much time to build his robot—only three and a half hours— and then it would be bedtime, which meant his parents

would be stopping by his bedroom to check on him. But for Bronson, unlike your average builder who might need a whole day or two, this would be plenty of time to get the job done.

So, with no further delay, Bronson began sifting through the cluttered toolshed to find the perfect parts to build his robot. He flipped open his laptop and searched for an old, unfinished robot design he and his friends had once started to develop. He studied the diagram and combined pieces of wood and a range of random junk parts to assemble the robot, including old computer parts, car parts, home appliances, electronic circuits, old springs, rusty pipes, metal gears, sheet metal, stereo speakers, and squeaky wheels.

As the hours passed by, Bronson hammered, cut, glued, soldered, twisted, scraped, screwed, bent, pried, adjusted, tweaked, programmed, and tested out his new creation.

He installed a rechargeable battery and computer drive that Myron had built inside the robot's solid log body made from a maple tree to give it life, and an AI program that Franny had developed to make his robot smart. And after attaching two sturdy arms and legs made of aspen, and hands and feet intricately fashioned from short, flexible willow branches, Bronson's new helper was finally complete.

Bronson flipped the robot's power switch on, and the blank screen on its small, beige computer-monitor head flickered on, displaying the robot's bright blue face and white pixelated eyes and mouth.

"Hello," said the robot with a smile.

"It's alive!" Bronson cackled like a mad

scientist. "I think I'll call you...Robot, for now, until I can think of a cooler name."

"How can I help you?" asked Robot.

"I'm so glad you asked," said Bronson. He unfolded a sheet of paper and read out loud his father's long list of chores to complete.

"We both better get some sleep, Robot, because we have a lot to do tomorrow." Bronson draped a dusty blue tarp over Robot and hurried back to the house just before his parents went up to his room to check on him.

— CHAPTER 4 —
THE CHORES

Bronson jumped out of bed early Saturday morning and hurried downstairs before anyone was awake. He wolfed down two pieces of aspen-bark toast before flying out the back door and heading to the toolshed. When he walked in, he was surprised by what he discovered.

"Robot, what did you do?" Bronson asked.

"Task number six: Clean and organize the toolshed," Robot replied.

Bronson had forgotten to power down Robot, so it had worked all through the night. The once messy and unorganized toolshed overflowing with junk was now tidy and in perfect order, with not an item out of place. Bronson suddenly realized his big idea was going to work even better than he'd imagined.

"Well, I think it's time to start showing you the ropes around here."

Bronson dressed Robot in one of his favorite red hoodies and a pair of his tan cargo pants. He pulled the hood over Robot's computer-monitor head and covered the screen with a brown wooden mask that he'd carved into his own likeness. Finally, before going back home to play Zombie Fight, Bronson gave Robot a quick tour of the lodge and strapped a pair of protective glasses over the wooden mask. The special glasses, equipped with a small Bluetooth video-camera, would deliver a live feed to a monitoring app on Bronson's phone.

This time, when Myron and Franny answered

Bronson's video chat and popped up on his computer screen, he was ready with his headset on and a big bowl of his favorite game-time snack by his side: BBQ birch-bark chips.

"Bronson, are you ready to play?" Myron asked.

"Are deep-fried, spicy crawdad nuggets your favorite game-time snack?" Bronson replied.

"Why yes, they are," Myron said as he popped a crawdad nugget into his mouth.

"So, your robot idea worked?" Franny asked.

"Are those caterpillar cheese puffs orange and fluffy like your fur?" Bronson answered.

"Why yes, they are!" Franny laughed as she chomped down on another one.

Bronson looked down at his robot-monitor app on his phone and saw Robot busy chopping wood. "Yep, it's hard at work as we speak,"

Bronson bragged. "It's programmed to go back to the toolshed when it's finished, or I can hit this 'home' button, and it will come directly to the location of my phone."

At that moment, Barry looked outside his bedroom window and saw Robot disguised as Bronson in the distance chopping wood, just as he had asked. "Well, it looks like Bronson is getting an early start on that list of chores I gave him," his father announced.

"See, and you thought he was going to try and stay in his room all day," Bronson's mother, Beverly, replied as she sat in front of her vanity, counting each stroke as she brushed her thick, luxurious dark brown fur. Beverly was a petite, energetic beaver with a bounce in her step, sparkling brown eyes, and a bright, endearing smile. Beverly was famous for wearing floral-patterned hooded jogging suits every day, and she followed a strict daily work schedule and grooming routine. These were all habits that she retained from her younger years of being a world-class competitive swimmer. She still held several local, national, and even world records in the sport.

"Well, I guess he proved me wrong," Barry said.

Meanwhile, just down the hall, Bronson was busy in his room fighting zombies with his friends.

By the end of the first day of the Zombie Fight tournament, Bronson and his friends were in first place and just one day away from winning the cash prize. Bronson watched Robot on his phone as it headed back to the toolshed.

"Mission accomplished," Bronson said before

turning off the monitoring app. "I have to put Robot back on its charger for the night, so I'll talk to you guys tomorrow morning."

Meanwhile, Bronson's parents were in the lodge's restaurant finishing up their prep work for the big pancake festival. Beverly glanced out an open window and spotted Robot heading back to the toolshed after its long day of hard work.

She called Bronson's name, but Robot kept walking and didn't respond. She turned to Barry, confused. "That was odd. Bronson just completely ignored me."

"He's probably just tired. I did give him a lot to do," Barry admitted. "I'll go talk to him just as soon as we finish up here."

When Bronson got to the toolshed, he slipped inside undetected. He was happy to discover that

Robot had already completed all but three chores on the list but was shocked by Robot's clothes. They were covered in paint, charcoal soot, and grass trimmings.

"Oh, Robot, you can't go back out looking like this tomorrow." Bronson quickly swapped clothes with Robot and connected it to the charger. But when he opened the door to leave, he was surprised by his father standing at the door getting ready to enter the toolshed.

"Bronson what on Earth happened to you?" his father asked, trying to see inside the toolshed. "And why didn't you answer your mother when she spoke to you earlier?"

Bronson quickly shut the toolshed door behind him. "Oh, hey…Dad. I-I-I must not have heard her."

"Well, that's what I figured. I'm sure you're

tired from working so hard today. Go get cleaned up and ready for dinner," Barry instructed. "I'm adding one more chore to your list tomorrow, and you'll need to be up early."

"Okay, you got it, Dad. What else do you need me to do?"

Barry handed Bronson a small key with a red, squishy foam keychain attached to it. "I want you to drive the ATV and trailer down to the Town Market tomorrow morning to pick up six big bags of flour for the Pancake Festival from Morgan Moose's Flour Mill."

Bronson was surprised by his father's request. The Town Market was a fixture in the valley, located in the heart of the community, between the big river and the old train tracks. It was just a short distance south from the lodge, down a winding, narrow road and canopied under a dense forest of giant pine trees. It featured a variety of water mill factories, food stands, and limestone shops and storefronts, which lined both sides of a narrow cobblestone road. You could find just about anything in the Town Market, from touristy trinkets and exotic food to everyday essentials.

It's where Barry got all his books from his favorite series, *Do It Yourself Like a Real Beaver*. Beverly stocked up there on her fruit- and flower-scented lotions and oils that kept her skin and fur so soft and luxurious. Bronson and his friends loved eating in the Town Market: Myron scarfed down spicy crawdad and fish tacos from his favorite food truck vendor, Franny enjoyed triple-scoop grasshopper and cricket flavored ice cream cones, and Bronson devoured the latest flavors at the Tree-Bark Jerky store.

"No problem, Dad. I got this," said Bronson.

"Thanks, son. I'm proud of you for taking care of your responsibilities. I know you wanted to play your video game all weekend."

"Speaking of that, what would you say if I told you I could build a robot to help out with the Pancake Festival tomorrow?" Bronson asked.

"No chance, Bronson," his father quickly rejected the idea. "This event is too important to leave in the hands of one of your new inventions."

"But what about the Pancake Maker Pro? It's helped improve the event, right?"

"Yes, it's a great invention and does help us do our work more efficiently, but it also took three years to perfect."

"But—"

"Do I need to remind you about all of the flour-fire flare-ups, maple syrup explosions, and whipped cream floods caused by the Pancake Maker Pro before it finally worked properly?"

"No, I remember," Bronson confessed. Maybe if he told his father about Robot and showed what Robot could do, he would understand. But just as Bronson put his paw on the door handle to open it, his father dropped the ultimate bombshell.

"Besides all of that, doing your work and taking care of your responsibilities is the Beaver way of life. We don't let others do our work if we can do it ourselves. It's the way every Beaver has lived since Barrett van Beaver, the founder and creator of Beaver Valley Lodge. That means NO ROBOT. Now go get cleaned up for dinner, son."

Bronson released the door handle of the toolshed and slowly retreated to the lodge. He went to his bedroom to share the news with his friends. Bronson was now unsure of what to do after hearing his father's speech about the Beaver way. He wanted to continue playing the video game with his friends. They'd been preparing for the tournament all year. But he felt guilty for being dishonest with his father.

Bronson woke up his computer, launched his video chat program, and called his friends. Myron and Franny quickly popped up on his screen.

"What's up, bro? Why do you have that look on your face?" Myron asked.

"Yeah, is everything okay?" Franny added.

"Yes and no," Bronson admitted. "You see, my dad just added another chore to my list.

This time he wants Robot, I mean me, to go down to the Town Market tomorrow morning at 6:30 a.m. to pick up six bags of flour for the Pancake Festival."

"So, what's the problem with that?" Myron replied. "Just enter the address into Robot's GPS, then upload an image of what the flour bags look like and let it do all the work so we can finish kicking some zombie booty and win the tournament."

"But it's a big responsibility," said Bronson.

"And it's a big paycheck for winning the tournament," Myron reminded Bronson, "which we need to help us build our dream workshop, remember?"

"Why don't you go yourself, Bronson?" said Franny as she strummed her guitar. "We don't start playing until 8:00 a.m., which gives you plenty of time to get there and back."

"No way!" Myron disagreed. "Why would he get up so early if he doesn't have to? We need Bronson well rested, so his mind is sharp and ready to play. I say send Robot and get an extra hour of sleep."

Bronson sat quietly for a moment with a blank stare on his face. He was conflicted with the idea of not living by the Beaver family way. "But that's not the Beaver way," he mumbled.

"What's not the Beaver way?" asked Franny.

"Letting someone else do your work and handle your responsibilities."

"So then go to the Town Market," Franny insisted.

"But I still have other chores on the list that I would need to do."

"I get it, Bronson," said Franny. "If you want to quit the team so you can finish your chores, we'll understand."

"Or just let Robot do all the work like it did today," said Myron. "You can make the same amount of money in two days as you could working at the lodge all summer. Surely, as a businessman, your dad would understand that."

"That's not fair, Myron," Franny defended.

"Quitting on your team's not fair either. You said it yourself, Franny," said Myron.

"That's not what I meant, and you know it," said Franny.

"Wait, let's not fight with each other," said Bronson. "Franny, I'm not going to quit on my team now. And you're right, Myron, if we can win this, my dad will probably be proud when he finds out how much money we earned.

I'm back in. Let's finish the tournament. I'll go back down to the toolshed tonight when my dad goes to bed and get Robot prepared for its big mission tomorrow morning."

— CHAPTER 5 —
THE TOWN MARKET MIX-UP

Peering down the long and dimly lit hallway through a crack in his bedroom door, Bronson waited patiently for his father to go to bed. Once his father had finally left his study and retreated to his bedroom, Bronson made his move. He snuck to the toolshed, and once there, he did just as Myron had suggested and programmed the address to Morgan Moose's Flour Mill into Robot's GPS.

"Hey, Robot, it's me again," Bronson whispered. "I need you to do something else for me tomorrow morning." He flipped open the makeshift control panel on Robot's chest and typed in the address. "This is a huge deal, and the whole town is counting on us. Please, don't mess it up."

"No problem. I got this," said Robot, sounding eerily like Bronson.

Bronson showed Robot the ATV and hitched a small trailer to it. He then handed Robot the ATV key. "Your mission is to drive this ATV and trailer down to the Town Market and pick up the flour for the Pancake Festival. You will need to leave at 6:30 a.m. and be back by 7:00 a.m. to load and start up the Pancake Maker Pro."

"I got this," Robot confirmed.

Bronson pointed to the dirt pathway behind the toolshed. "This ravine path will take you all the way there. But be careful. It's a rocky, winding path, so take your time and don't rush,

THE TOWN MARKET MIX-UP

or you could risk tipping over the trailer and spilling the flour or, worse yet, wrecking the ATV down the side of the ravine. Got it?"

"I got this," Robot repeated.

Bronson next showed Robot an empty, yellow fifty-pound flour bag. "When you arrive, there will be six bags of flour that look something like this waiting for you."

"I will collect six fifty-pound bags that look something like this."

"Robot, I think you got this!" Bronson said. "Now, for the final step, let's head over to the restaurant and I'll show you how to load and turn on the Pancake Maker Pro!"

"Sounds awesome," said Robot.

"Oh, it is awesome, Robot. It is!"

By the time Bronson finished training Robot, he was tired. But instead of going to bed so

he could be well-rested and mentally sharp—
as Myron had suggested—he decided to chug
a tall can of Energy Blast and stay up all night
playing Zombie Fight until finally falling
asleep at 4:30 a.m. It was a terrible decision
that Bronson would soon regret.

At 6:30 a.m., while Bronson was fast asleep,
Robot powered up and headed out on its
mission. The low growl of the ATV's engine
woke Bronson's father just long enough for him
to get up and stagger across the bedroom to the
window and see Robot driving away.

"*That's* my boy," Barry mumbled before
returning to his bed and going back to sleep.

Slowly but surely, Robot guided the ATV
down the dark and narrow rocky path heading
toward the Town Market, stopping only a few
times for early-bird hikers and joggers from

the valley to pass by. Robot eventually arrived at the Town Market just before the crack of dawn and right on schedule. But there was a big problem waiting, a major kink in Bronson's plan that he had not anticipated. The Town Market had just begun doing sidewalk repairs in front of all the shops. The flour mill's once old, cracked, and weed-filled sidewalk was now a freshly poured, perfectly smooth, shiny slab of wet concrete. However, the nightshift beaver crew had just left for a break, and no barricades were surrounding the sidewalk to prevent anyone from walking on it.

Instead, there was a huge sign, intended for Bronson, with big red letters hanging in the front door's window that read: "CAUTION WET CONCRETE! BRONSON, THE FLOUR IS LOCATED ON THE BACK DOCK." But

Robot wasn't programmed to read, so it didn't know to go to the back of the store to find the bags of flour. Robot instead spotted six similar-looking yellow bags of cement powder sitting on the wobbly front steps of the flour mill. Not knowing any better, Robot hopped off the ATV and stamped through the freshly poured concrete and up the shaky stairs to retrieve the six bags. One by one, it grabbed each fifty-pound bag and tossed it onto the trailer, and each time it marched back through the wet concrete and left a trail of deep footprints behind. When it was finished loading the bags on the trailer, the perfect new sidewalk was a messy puddle of gray mud. As Robot started to head back to the lodge with the loaded trailer, two hefty nightshift beaver workers returning from their break spotted Robot as it was driving away.

"Hey kid, what are you doing?" one worker yelled after seeing the destroyed sidewalk and realizing the remaining bags of concrete were gone.

But Robot didn't stop; it just kept driving up the path and into the woods.

"I know who you are, kid!" said the other worker, "and you're in big trouble for this!"

Robot made it back to the lodge with all six bags of concrete powder intact while Bronson and the rest of the lodge remained asleep. It backed the trailer up to the restaurant's back door, went inside, and started up Bronson's great invention: the Pancake Maker Pro. It was slightly larger than a double door refrigerator, a colossus work of engineering perfection with its complex mechanical inner workings neatly hidden from sight by its heavy-duty, red metal casing. It had a giant gray metal funnel on top, which was used for pouring entire bags of flour into the machine, so it could continuously mix, cook, and plate delicious, fluffy, golden brown pancakes in stacks of three and automatically top them with a big hunk of creamy yellow butter and a generous pour of warm maple syrup. And with a push of a button on a small control panel, the pancakes could be customized with the customer's choice of whipped cream, chocolate chips, blueberries, strawberries, or bananas.

Like a soldier following marching orders, Robot ripped open each bag of cement, climbed the little green stepladder next to the pancake machine, and dumped all six bags into the device through its large funnel on top. The other ingredients that made up the secret Beaver family pancake recipe—including baking powder, salt, sugar, eggs, milk, and vanilla—had been carefully measured, mixed, and preloaded the night before by Beverly. To complete its mission, Robot turned the temperature setting knob from chill to cook, pressed the big green start button, and left the restaurant's kitchen the same way it had come in.

Meanwhile, as the pancake machine was slowly mixing the ingredients, Bronson's parents, now both fully awake, were drinking their morning coffee at the main lodge.

"Well, I better get over to the restaurant," said Beverly. "I have a few things to finish getting ready."

Just then, the phone rang, and Barry nearly fell off his stool hustling over to answer it. "This is probably him," he said with excitement.

The famous food critic, Bardo J. Bear, was supposed to call that morning to get directions to the lodge.

"Then we need to hurry if we're going to have everything perfect before he arrives," said Beverly as she hurried out the front door of the lodge.

But when she arrived at the restaurant and walked into the kitchen, she was shocked to see that things were far from perfect.

The pancake machine was smoking, rattling, and rolling out plates of rock-solid cement pancakes.

"Oh, my goodness, no, this can't be!" Beverly gasped just before the sputtering machine came to a jolting stop. The Pancake Maker Pro was frozen like a museum statue from moving the thick cement through its most essential gears, pulleys, and sprockets.

"Bronson!" she belted. "What did you do?"

She followed the trail of fresh cement footsteps leading out the back door of the restaurant to discover Robot marching steadily across the green meadow back to the toolshed.

"Bronson!" she called out. "I know you can hear me!"

"I got this," replied Robot as it stepped inside the toolshed and slammed the door behind it.

"Oh, you are in big trouble for this. I'm going to get your father right now," Beverly yelled as she stormed back over to the lodge to tell Barry.

Meanwhile, back in the lodge, Barry's phone call was not going well, either. On the other end wasn't a hungry Mr. Bear as he expected, but an angry Mr. Moose, who told Barry the far-from-perfect news about Bronson's flour mill mishap earlier that morning.

Barry slammed down the phone. "Unbelievable!" He marched upstairs toward Bronson's room with Beverly now trailing closely behind him.

Just then, Bronson was slowly waking up. He yawned big and immediately started up his computer and called Franny and Myron to video chat. Both quickly popped up on his screen, already waiting to play.

"Late night?" Franny asked.

"Bro, you look like moose poop," Myron added.

"Sorry guys, I guess I stayed up too late," Bronson answered.

"So how did Robot do today?" Franny asked.

"I'm not sure," Bronson nervously replied as he searched for his phone.

"No worries, bro. Just see if it hit all the checkpoints on the GPS map," Myron suggested.

"Good idea," replied Bronson, looking at his phone. "Cool, it looks like it hit all of the checkpoints on time and is now back in the toolshed. I can just send it back out to finish up my last three chores remotely with the app."

"Then let the games begin!" Myron cheered.

At that moment, Bronson's door flung open. There stood Beverly and Barry, both very angry, confused, and disappointed with Bronson.

"I just got off the phone with Mr. Moose at the flour mill, and he said you never picked up the six bags of flour, but you did manage to destroy his new sidewalk and steal six bags of cement."

"Wait. What?" Bronson replied.

"And then you ruined the Pancake Maker Pro by filling it with the cement that you stole," said Beverly.

"WHAT?" Bronson and his father yelled together in disbelief.

Bronson picked up his phone to try and watch the video playback of Robot's mission to see what happened, but his father quickly snatched it from him. As his father took the phone, Bronson's finger accidentally pressed the home button signaling Robot to go directly to the phone's current location.

"Your phone and video game playing days are officially over," his father said as he tossed Bronson's phone on his computer desk. "Let's go, son! I need to see how much damage you did at the restaurant."

"So do I," Bronson mumbled under his breath.

"We only have thirty minutes before the doors open to the public," Beverly said. "And we have to have the first plate ready for the food critic sooner than that."

So Bronson, Beverly, and Barry all headed back to the restaurant together, leaving Franny and Myron alone in the room on Bronson's computer screen.

"Well, that stinks," Myron said, breaking the awkward silence.

"Yes, yes it does," Franny replied.

"So does this mean he won't be playing with us today?" Myron asked.

"Yes, yes it does, Myron," Franny repeated.

"Okay, just checking."

— CHAPTER 6 —
THE PANCAKE FESTIVAL

As the locals throughout the valley were waking up early that spring morning and getting their taste buds ready to feast on the best pancakes in the world, Bronson and his parents stared in shock at the silent and motionless Pancake Maker Pro covered in gray concrete. At the same time last year, this industrious and undisputed world-record-holding pancake-making machine had the entire kitchen filled with the sweet smell of maple syrup and warm pancakes.

"Why did you do this, son?" Barry asked. "Are you mad at us for some reason?"

Bronson opened his mouth but couldn't speak.

"Can you fix it?" asked Beverly.

Bronson, nearly in tears, stood as frozen as his greatest invention, saying nothing.

"Bronson, stop ignoring your mother and say something!" his father demanded.

"I didn't do this," replied Bronson.

"What?" exclaimed both of his parents.

"I saw you with my own eyes, Bronson Beaver," said Beverly with her hands on her hips.

"It wasn't me," Bronson said.

Just then, Robot had finally found its way to the main lodge. Finding Bronson's phone inside his bedroom, it sat down at his computer desk and said, "home," just before shutting itself down.

Back at the restaurant, Bronson had a lot of explaining to do.

"What do you mean you didn't do this, son?" said Barry. "I saw you leave to go to the market this morning, and your mother just saw you leaving the restaurant."

"It was Robot, okay?" Bronson finally confessed. "I built a robot so that I could play in the Zombie Fight tournament with Franny and Myron this weekend so we could win the prize money and build a new workshop. I disguised it in my clothes and programmed it to do all my chores, and it was going great the first day. But then something must have gone wrong at the Town Market this morning for it to have brought back bags of cement instead of flour."

"Nice try, son," replied Barry. "That won't get you out of trouble for this."

"Well, that would explain why he was ignoring me," said Beverly.

"Where is this so-called robot now?" asked Barry.

"It's in the toolshed," answered Bronson. "I can show you if you want."

Just as they started walking toward the toolshed, the restaurant phone rang. They also noticed in the distance a crowd from town making their way toward the lodge.

Beverly and Barry both raced back to the restaurant to answer the phone.

"Hello," Beverly said into the phone. "Yes, he's right here. One moment." She covered the receiver and whispered, "It's the food critic."

Barry slapped his forehead and paced back and forth twice before finally taking the phone. "Eh-hem, Mr. Bear, how are you? Oh, yes, you are very close. Just continue traveling down Big River Road about two miles, take a left turn at Green Meadow Lane, and we are one mile past Beaver Bridge on the right side. You can't miss our freshly painted sign." He hung up the phone. "We're finished."

"Let's not give up. Maybe we can still figure something out," said Beverly.

By now, the early-bird pancake-lovers were beginning to line up and gather around the front door of the lodge restaurant, looking through the windows and drooling at the empty dining room.

"Let me try to go back to the Town Market and get the flour, Dad," Bronson said.

"He's probably five minutes away, Bronson," replied his father. "It takes fifteen minutes just to get over to the Town Market."

Bronson ran to the toolshed and jumped on the ATV, still determined to race to the Town Market and bring back the flour they needed, but the ATV's foot shifter was covered with hard concrete and wouldn't shift into first gear. Bronson quickly decided to take the lodge's motorized fishing boat down the big river, which passed right beside the Town Market. He hustled around to the other side of the restaurant and found the fishing boat resting peacefully by the dock in the big blue lake, but just before he could get in, he heard a deep and unfamiliar voice.

"Excuse me, I believe I'm a bit lost. Could you tell me where I can find The Bear Claw restaurant?" said the voice.

Bronson gulped and slowly turned around to discover the world-famous food critic Bardo J.

Bear looking at him. He was a large, serious-looking bear wearing a forest green three-piece suit, lime green shirt, and maroon bowtie. His golden-brown fur was thick and shiny and parted perfectly down the middle of his head.

"Um, yeah, it's right this way," said Bronson. "Follow me."

Bronson and Mr. Bear navigated their way through the hungry and restless crowd waiting outside. As they stepped into the restaurant, Beverly immediately greeted Mr. Bear and guided him to a table with the best view of the lake and mountains. Bronson quickly brought him their popular breakfast drink options, including a tall glass of cold spring water, a short glass of freshly-squeezed orange juice, and a heaping mug of hot cocoa with fluffy white marshmallows.

Bronson and his mother returned to the restaurant's kitchen to find Barry rifling through the cabinets looking for any trace of extra flour.

"We don't even have enough flour here to make one pancake," said Barry. "The jig is up. I guess I'll go out there and tell him the truth so we don't waste any more of his time. There goes The Bear Claw's five-star review *and* our credibility." Barry walked slowly toward the dining room to deliver Mr. Bear the regretful news.

"No, Dad, let me tell him," Bronson insisted. "Besides, this whole thing is my fault for not being honest anyway."

But before Bronson could say another word, the back door of the restaurant flew open and in ran Franny Fox.

"Am I too late?" Franny asked while panting and flipping hot pancakes between two strange-looking frying pans. "I ran all the way so you could serve these pancakes to that famous food critic."

Bronson and his parents looked at each other with confusion.

"Franny, you ran all the way here from your house, flipping those pancakes?" Barry asked.

Franny nodded her head yes while continuing to juggle the pancakes between the sizzling frying pans.

"But how did you cook them with no heat?" Beverly asked.

"Remember that portable solar-powered frying pan prototype Bronson and I invented?" Franny explained. "Well, I figured this would be the perfect time to test them out, and guess what? They work!"

"But wait, Mr. Bear came to try *our* famous pancake recipe, not yours, Franny." Barry said.

"This *is* your recipe."

"*Really*—how did you get it?"

"Bronson's robot."

"Oh, no, not that robot again."

"Oh, yes. Since it was in Bronson's bedroom in front of his computer, I could see it from my computer in the chat window Bronson left open. When I spoke to Robot, it powered up. I told it to go downstairs and get the recipe from Mrs. Beaver's recipe box and send me a photo of it. I hope you don't mind."

"Not at all. That was very clever, Franny," said Beverly.

"Thank you!" Franny said with a big smile.

"Well, what are we waiting for?" asked Barry. "Let's get those pancakes on a plate with some butter and syrup, Bronson."

"But what about the others?" Beverly said, pointing to the crowd waiting outside the front door.

Just then, the back door of the restaurant flew open once again. This time it was Myron Mink. His legs were trembling as he strained to carry a fifty-pound bag of flour on his shoulders.

"A little help here," he gasped.

"What are you trying to do, break your skinny neck, Myron?" Barry asked as he helped him set the bag of flour down.

"There are five more bags where this one came from outside," Myron said before collapsing to the ground from exhaustion.

They all looked out the back door of the

restaurant and, sure enough, stacked up in the back of Myron's mint green, rusty, vintage Volkswagen van, there were the remaining five bags of flour they needed to feed the masses.

"Myron, I take back everything I ever said about you being lazy," said Barry.

"Awesome. I appreciate that, Mr. B…wait, you think I'm lazy?"

"Myron, how did you pull this off and get here so quickly?" Bronson asked.

"It was easy, bro," Myron replied. "Since I already live close by the Town Market, I drove there and convinced a very grumpy Mr. Moose at the flour mill to allow me the honor of delivering his amazing high-quality flour to such a delicious event dedicated to helping establish solidarity and unity within our fine community. Next thing I knew, two of his workers were loading up the ole green boogie mobile, then I took a few secret shortcuts to get here in record time. The end."

"Well, Franny and Myron, since the Pancake Maker Pro is down, and you're already here, can we count on you to help us the rest of the way?" Barry asked.

"It would be an honor," replied Franny.

"How much do you pay?" Myron asked with a smile.

"Myron!" Franny interrupted.

"What? I'm kidding. Of course, I'm here to help my best bud," Myron said as he fist-bumped Bronson.

"All right, let's get cooking then. Doors will open to the community in exactly six minutes," said Barry.

Beverly burst through the swinging kitchen

doors coming from the dining room, holding a clean plate. "Mr. Bear likes them! We need another short stack, and quick!"

Together they formed a pancake assembly line and kept everyone fed all day. Myron mixed the batter and bussed tables, Bronson and his father worked the griddle, and Franny and Beverly plated the pancakes, added the toppings, and served in the dining room. It was real teamwork at its finest.

The day turned to night by the time they flipped the last pancake and the dining room was finally empty. They didn't break any new records, but they did enjoy feeling a great sense of accomplishment for sticking together and overcoming a bad situation. Plus, the lodge received the highest rating and best review possible from Bardo J. Bear, who vowed to return next time with his friends and family.

Bronson, Franny, and Myron took off their white aprons and walked outside together to get some fresh air.

"I don't think I had a chance to thank you two for doing this," Bronson said with tears welling in his eyes. "I would have ruined my family's business and reputation if you two hadn't come to help us. You both gave up your day of playing our favorite video game and your chance of winning the tournament to help me."

"Bro, don't get all mushy on us, all right? That's what friends are supposed to do," Myron said, slugging Bronson in his arm.

"We shouldn't have pressured you to play in

the tournament when you had more important responsibilities," said Franny.

"We? Do you have a mouse in your pocket?" Myron joked.

"What are you talking about?" Franny frowned.

"You said *we*, so I said do you have a mouse in your pock—"

"Myron, why would I have a mouse in my pocket? Ew, that's not funny, it's gross!"

"What do you mean it's not funny? It's funny. See you said *we* pressured Bronson to play, but I don't agree that *I* pressured him to play, so when you say *we* you must be saying you and someone else other than *me*, perhaps a tiny little mouse friend you have named Mookie, who's chillin' in your pocket," Myron rambled on. "Therefore, you and Mookie would be the *we* who pressured Bronson to play. Get it?" Myron giggled alone until his desperate laughter quickly faded back to the sound of crickets chirping in the cool night air.

"A mouse in my pocket named Mookie. That's the joke? No, I don't get it," Franny confirmed.

"Okay, how about *Mitch*!" Myron suggested. "Is the name Mitch better?"

"Sorry, dude, it's just a bad joke with either name," Bronson concluded with a sympathetic laugh. "But seriously, like I was saying, I just didn't want to let you guys down."

"Which is the same exact reason why we came to help you. It's all for one and one for all," said Myron.

"That's right," Franny agreed. "Besides, there will be other Zombie Fight tournaments later this year, but there's only one Beaver Valley Pancake Festival every year."

"Speaking of that, I better get going," Myron said. "I want to get in a quick game before I go to bed. Anyone else?"

"No, I'm way too exhausted," replied Franny, "but I could use a lift home if you don't mind."

"Well, I definitely can't play tonight," said Bronson. "I'll be washing that mountain of dishes and silverware by hand all night."

"Disgusting," Franny blurted out.

"Yep, that plus no video games for a month is part of my punishment for being dishonest and skipping out on my responsibilities, my dad said. Plus, I'll have to work to help replace the six bags of cement that Robot took and repair the damages to the sidewalk, the ATV, and whatever it's done to my bedroom by now."

The three laughed together.

— CHAPTER 7 —
THE BEAVER WAY

B ronson watched his friends drive away and then went back into the restaurant to start washing the never-ending pile of dishes waiting for him. Alone, Bronson finally had time to think about the choices he'd made that had caused him so much trouble, and he decided he would never again avoid his responsibilities at the lodge.

He worked tirelessly into the night until all the dishes were finally clean before sitting down at a table in the dining room to roll the silverware with the lodge's monogrammed, white cloth napkins. After some time of doing this, Bronson began dozing off. "Jeez, I'm getting sleepy," he said while straining to keep his heavy eyelids open. "Just a few more and then I can go to my room and crash."

But when he looked back up, he was startled to see his father suddenly sitting at the table across from him.

"Whoa, Dad, I thought you were back at the lodge," Bronson said as he jumped up from the table, nearly knocking over the pile of neatly rolled silverware.

Barry was wearing an old gray wool driving cap and winding up an antique gold pocket watch. There was a dusty deck of playing cards sitting on the table, too. He just grinned at Bronson and picked up the deck of cards. "Do you know who this hat, pocket watch, and playing cards belonged to?"

"No, I don't. Should I?" Bronson replied.

"Barrett van Beaver," Barry said.

"My grandfather's grandfather, right?"

"That's right. The founder and creator of the lodge, the restaurant, *and* the Town Market."

"Wow, those are pretty old, then." Bronson sat back down at the table to get a closer look.

"Oh, yes."

"Why are you showing them to me?"

"Because you are just like him," said Barry.

"I am?"

"Yes. Barrett, *like you*, possessed exceptional gifts of imagination and ingenuity. And he *also* loved to hang out with his pals and play games in his free time."

"Seriously?" Bronson's eyes widened with curiosity.

"Seriously. Not only did Barrett work hard and love to invent and build, but he also loved to play a card game called bridge with his friends."

"Really? That's so cool." Bronson stopped folding the silverware and examined the deck of cards. "These were really his cards?"

"Yes, that was his favorite deck of cards, and this was his lucky hat and gold watch, which brings me to the point I wanted to make," Barry said as he carefully set the watch down on the table and slid it over to Bronson.

"Okay, I think I know where you're going with this."

"I didn't ground you from playing your game for a month because I don't like you playing video games. I grounded you because you chose to play your game over personally taking care of your responsibilities and doing the work with your own two paws."

"I know, Dad," Bronson said with his head down. "It's not the Beaver way."

"That's right. You want free time to relax and hang out with your friends, and video games do that for you. Just like a game of bridge did that for Barrett, and reading books in my study does that for me. But Barrett kept this watch to tell him when it was time to stop playing and get back to the business of being a Beaver, by being productive and helping others."

Barry flipped the gold watch over to show Bronson an inscription on the back that read: *Be brave. Be productive. Be helpful.*

"I feel terrible for being dishonest and straying from the Beaver way," said Bronson.

"Don't feel terrible. Just invent things to help you and others work smarter and faster. Not so you don't have to work."

"Like the Pancake Maker Pro?"

"Exactly."

"I guess I just wanted to win the prize money so bad that I lost sight of the Beaver way."

"No amount of money should do that. How much was it?"

"Three thousand dollars."

"In two days! Well, maybe it *is* time for us Beavers to find a new way."

"Dad!"

"I'm kidding," Barry chuckled. "The good news is, you and your friends still have all summer to earn enough money to build your new workshop before next winter."

"How? Franny only babysits part-time, and Myron has never had a summer job."

"Well, maybe we can see if Myron and Franny

want to help us around the lodge and restaurant this summer," Barry suggested.

"Seriously? That's a great idea, Dad!"

The two continued to talk and fold the silverware together until the last knife and fork were finally out of sight.

Bright and early the next morning, a loud horn followed by laughter woke Bronson abruptly from a bad dream, causing him to gasp for air in a panic. In his dream, his father had just caught him playing Zombie Fight with Franny and Myron, despite being grounded from the game.

He lay quietly, staring at the ceiling and happy to be awake and know it was only a dream until he realized he could still hear the sound effects from the game. Bronson sat up and saw Robot sitting at his desk playing Zombie Fight with Franny and Myron.

"There he is," Myron shouted.

"It's about time, sleepyhead," said Franny.

"What is happening right now?" Bronson asked.

"Bro, your robot is a beast at Zombie Fight," said Myron.

"A what at what?" Bronson asked.

"Robot is amazing at Zombie Fight," said Franny.

"I got this!" Robot shouted.

"Yeah, you do, Robot!" Myron shouted back.

"I must still be dreaming," Bronson said as he sat on his bed and watched Robot playing his video game.

"We're not sure how Robot learned the game, but he's freaking awesome," Myron laughed.

"Robot single-handedly helped our team get third place in the tournament yesterday while we were at the Pancake Festival," said Franny.

"Yeah, and we would've received the $650 third-place prize," Myron said, "but they figured out it was a robot and disqualified us."

"Unbelievable," Bronson said.

At that moment, Beverly knocked on Bronson's bedroom door. "Bronson, your father is waiting in his truck for you," she shouted from the other side of the door.

Bronson leaped off his bed and tried to turn off his computer, but his mother opened the door and stepped inside before he could get there.

"Oh, my goodness! What's going on in here?"

"Mom, I'd like you to meet Robot."

"So this is the infamous Robot?" Beverly

asked as she slowly stepped back into the doorway, bumping into Barry who had come back inside to see what was keeping Bronson.

"It won't hurt you, Mom," Bronson laughed.

"Where's that cement-stealing bandit-of-a-robot?" said Barry, who was wearing his work clothes—an old pair of blue overalls and a red plaid shirt.

He squeezed past Beverly and entered Bronson's bedroom to get a closer look.

"It plays video games, too?" Barry asked.

"Apparently," Bronson replied.

"Well, not today," Barry announced. "It's going to help us fix the sidewalk down at the market."

"But I thought you said—"

"I said, *help* us, not do it for us. Robot is going to stir the cement and keep it coming while we pour and finish the new sidewalk," Barry further explained.

"Sounds fun!" said Myron as he chomped down on a spicy crawdad nugget while watching and listening from the computer.

"Then you can help us," Barry replied.

"Well, I'm in too then," said Franny.

"Cool! Dad, can they both help us?" asked Bronson

"They sure can. The more, the merrier," assured Barry.

"This is so awesome! I'm definitely in," Myron announced. "You're going to need someone to handle the heavy lifting," he said while flexing his boney arms.

Everyone shared a good laugh.

That day, Bronson and his friends worked hard alongside Robot and Barry until late afternoon when the job was finally complete. They laughed, smiled, and had a good time in the process. Bronson learned that hard work was much more enjoyable with friends.

Just before they returned home, Barry had one last item of business to take care of.

"Great work today, gang," Barry said. "I'm really impressed with your chemistry together. In fact, I'm so impressed I'd like to officially offer you, Franny, and you, Myron, positions at the lodge for your summer jobs."

Myron leaped off the ground with excitement. "Seriously? Yes! Wait, am I dreaming? Somebody pinch me...not too hard, though."

Franny welled up with joy. "Oh, my goodness, yes, I'd love to work at the lodge this summer."

"Now hold on, I haven't even told you what your jobs will be," Barry said.

"It doesn't matter!" Franny exclaimed, unable to contain her excitement. "Any job at the lodge will be better than babysitting another summer for Patty Porcupine's quadruplets."

"What's so bad about that job?" asked Barry.

"Oh, they're a family of huggers, Mr. B," Myron answered with a straight face.

"Yeah, it's true." Franny agreed with a pained look.

"Okay, well, in that case, you're going to love being our restaurant's new assistant manager."

"Really? That is so cool! I would absolutely love that job!" Franny jumped up and hugged Barry, squeezing him so hard that he gasped and couldn't move his arms that were pinned to his sides. "Thank you so much!"

"Uh, I don't think Mr. B's a hugger, Franny," Myron said.

"I don't think he's breathing," said Bronson. "Dad, breathe!"

"Right. I'm so sorry!" Franny quickly released Barry and fixed his clothes.

Barry composed himself, cleared his throat, and turned to Myron. "Myron, since you're the only one old enough to drive and you know your way around the valley so well, you'll be our official shuttle driver. Your job will be to show our guests around the valley and take them to and from the Town Market and train station."

"Woohoo—I got a job! My parents won't believe it!" Myron shouted. "I'm the official shuttle driver for the Beaver Valley Lodge!" His joyful voice pierced the quiet late afternoon air and echoed through the valley treetops.

— CHAPTER 8 —
THE WORKSHOP

That summer would turn out to be the best summer of Bronson's young life. He and his friends got to hang out together every day at work. During their breaks, they would laugh, joke, and brainstorm invention ideas. And by summer's end, they were finally able to build their more spacious, state-of-the-art, dream workshop with the money they earned from working at the lodge.

And the new workshop was everything they'd imagined. It was bright and cozy due to its wall-to-wall app-integrated LED shop lights and smart heating and cooling system. It featured three brand new workbenches, so they each had their own station to work from; an entire wall dedicated to their special tools; a separate area with alphabetized organizational bins, lockers, and shelves which neatly housed their building materials out of sight until needed; a lunch table and fridge, so they could refuel their minds and bodies with food and drinks without ever having to leave their shop; and, of course, a big-screen TV with a gaming console so they could play Zombie Fight to help them relax their creative minds from time to time.

During the chillier months of autumn, Bronson, Franny, and Myron would meet every weekend to hang out and work on the new ideas they had dreamed up together during the summer.

But with their bigger and better workshop soon came bigger and better goals and dreams, as Myron suddenly discovered one quiet Saturday afternoon in September. While he was searching on his phone for a 3D printer for the workshop, he stumbled upon something much better.

"Hey, you guys, check this out! Our town is accepting entries for a national youth inventor team competition! And get this—first prize is the Mega Maker 3D printer!"

Franny stopped writing code on her laptop and peeked her head around the screen. "Isn't that the exact one we want for the workshop?"

Bronson stopped sketching out a new idea at his workbench and hurried across the workshop to see Myron's phone screen. "Did you say an invention competition?"

"Yes. And that's not all." Myron continued

reading. "The winners will be featured in *Inventor Illustrated.*"

"Bronson, that's your favorite magazine!" Franny exclaimed. "You've always dreamed of being in that magazine."

Bronson couldn't believe what he was hearing. His imagination was churning so fast he was feeling lightheaded.

Myron kept scrolling and reading more. "Whoa, it says the finalist will get an all-expenses-paid trip to Invention City for the award ceremony."

"Hey, Franny, you've always dreamed of visiting Invention City," Bronson remembered.

Franny's face lit up with excitement. "What's the competition called?"

"The *Invention City Challenge* and the registration deadline is...today!"

"Done! I'm going to their site and registering us as a team right now," Franny said as she rapidly tapped the keys on her laptop.

"It looks like we only have one month left to submit a prototype," Myron said.

"I guess we better get to work then," said Franny.

"We're going to build our best invention *ever* for this," Bronson announced. "No offense, Robot."

"You got this!" Robot blurted out with a pixelated smile as it busily swept the workshop floor.

"No, *we* got this," replied Bronson.

They all three nodded their heads in agreement, Franny hit the send button on the registration form, and together they whooped, cheered, and danced around the workshop filled with joy and excitement.

The End

CPSIA information can be obtained
at www.ICGtesting.com
Printed in the USA
BVHW071224080421
604475BV00004B/487